Puppy Mudge Takes a Bath

By Cynthia Rylant

Illustrated by Isidre Mones

in the style of Suçie Stevenson

READY-TO-READ

ALADDIN PAPERBACKS

New York   London   Toronto   Sydney   Singapore

First Aladdin Paperbacks edition April 2004

Text copyright © 2002 by Cynthia Rylant
Illustrations copyright © 2002 by Suçie Stevenson

ALADDIN PAPERBACKS
An imprint of Simon & Schuster Children's Publishing Division
1230 Avenue of the Americas
New York, NY 10020

READY-TO-READ is a registered trademark of Simon & Schuster.

Book design by Mark Siegel
The text of this book is set in Goudy.
Manufactured in the United States of America
20 19 18 17 16

Also available in a Simon & Schuster Books for Young Readers hardcover edition.

The Library of Congress has cataloged the hardcover edition as follows:
Rylant, Cynthia.
Puppy Mudge takes a bath / by Cynthia Rylant; illustrated by Suçie Stevenson.
p. cm.
Summary: When his puppy Mudge gets dirty, Henry has some trouble giving him a bath.
ISBN-13: 978-0-689-83980-1 (hc.)
ISBN-10: 0-689-83980-4 (hc.)
[1. Dogs—Fiction. 2. Baths—Fiction.] I. Stevenson, Suçie, ill. II. Title
PZ7.R982 Hm 2001
[E]—dc21
00-052234
ISBN-13: 978-0-689-86621-0 (pbk.)
ISBN-10: 0-689-86621-6 (pbk.)
1111 LAK

This is Henry.

This is Henry's puppy Mudge.
Mudge loves mud.

Mud makes Mudge roll.

And roll.
And roll.

Mudge is muddy.
Mudge needs a bath.

There is the tub.

Where is Mudge?

Mudge is hiding.
Mudge does not love tubs.

Henry finds Mudge.

Mudge is in the tub.

Now Henry is in the tub!
Mudge is happy.

Mudge is very clean.
Henry is very clean.

The tub is very muddy!

Henry and Mudge dry off.
They go back outside.

Look what Mudge found.

Mudge is smelly.

Mudge needs a bath.

There is the tub.

Where is Mudge?

Here we go again.

OBSOLETE